W9-DCC-401

JUST A QUILT?
Copyright © 2008 Dalen Keys
ISBN 978-1-886068-34-6
Library of Congress Control Number: 2008942006

Published by Fruitbearer Publishing, LLC
P.O. Box 777, Georgetown, DE 19947
(302) 856-6649 • FAX (302) 856-7742
www.fruitbearer.com • fruitbearer.publishing@verizon.net
Illustrated by Kim Sponaugle
Edited by Pam Halter

Printed in the United States of America

DEDICATED TO

Mitzie, my wife the quilter,
and
Chase, my son

"Chase," Mommy called.
"It's time to leave for Grandma's house."

Chase charged into the kitchen
with his backpack and suitcase.
"Okay, Mommy. I'm ready!"

"Did you pack everything I laid out for you?"

Chase nodded.
"Yup, I packed everything."

As Mommy set her cup of coffee on the saucer,
she saw the corner of Chase's favorite quilt
sticking out of his backpack.
"Did you pack your quilt too?" Mommy asked.

Chase frowned.
"But Mommy, I don't have a quilt!"

Mommy's eyebrows raised in surprise.
"You don't?"

"Nope," Chase said with a little grin.

"You might think I have a quilt, Mommy,"
Chase said.
"But really, it's a busy, busy airport
for all my airplanes."

"I don't have a quilt.
I have a huge race track for my fast cars."

"When I'm a superhero —
I have my cape."

"When I'm fighting
huge fire-breathing dragons,
I have my thick armor to protect me."

"It's not a quilt!
It's a deep, dark cave —
and I'm a brave explorer."

"Sometimes it's my
very own flying carpet
when I fly high over old, magical cities."

"Or, it's my saddle
when I am a cowboy
riding on my horse during a starlit night."

"It's my tent
when I'm on a safari in Africa."

"See, Mommy? It's not just a quilt!"

"That's good to know," Mommy said.
"When I made it, I thought it was just a quilt.
I'm glad you told me.
I can see that it is much more than just a quilt."

Mommy gave Chase a big hug.

As Mommy held out her hand
to count on her fingers, she said,
"In that case, maybe you should get

your busy airport,
your race track,
your superhero cape,
your secret shield,
your thick armor,
your deep dark cave,
your flying carpet,
your saddle,
and your safari tent,

just in case you need them
at Grandma's house tonight."

Chase's smile went all the way to his eyes.
"I already did, Mommy."
"They're right here in my backpack."

Then he added,
"Besides, Mommy, you know I can't sleep at night
without my quilt!"